Martha

-

The Girl

with

a Rabbit

Heart

Martha

-

The Girl

with

a Rabbit

Heart

Patsy Toe

To my mum and dad
with love.

*

Her name was Martha. She was the daughter of the north cloud and the eastern wind. She was born on the edge of two worlds – the one you call earth and the one above your head. It was called Cloudiotropia. Martha was a petite, hazel-eyed girl with long, straight, black hair hanging down to her shoulders. She was neither tall nor short. She always wore short, blue dresses and tights with black-and-yellow stripes. On her feet, she wore heavy black boots.

Before I tell you her story, I must explain something.

Every newborn cloud-child is born without a heart, and it is up to the parents to decide what kind of heart they are going to have. Most of them choose a lion or bear heart to make their children brave, or an eagle heart if they want them to be fast and majestic. But Martha's parents somehow decided to choose a rabbit heart for her. A tiny, little, scared, and shy rabbit heart. Can you imagine? What a strange choice. What could she do with it in her life? She could not understand why they had done it, and sometimes she was very angry at them, but she could not do anything about it.

Ten years had passed in Cloudiotropia since Martha's birth. On this day, she was sitting and peeking from behind her favourite cloud into others' lives below. Everyone, people, animals, and birds, seemed to be having adventures and friends. You cannot imagine how jealous she was. But whenever she tried to do or say something to someone, she felt her little rabbit heart inside her chest. She wanted to run from everyone and everything. She really wished to be brave and have courage, but it seemed to be impossible for her. So, Martha was alone and, believe me, very unhappy.

1

**

It was the beginning of summer; a time when thunderstorm clouds grow bigger and bigger. Martha had just finished her morning tea when she spotted a rabbit family with a few little bunnies. They looked like they wanted to cross the glade in the forest but a big, brown-feathered falcon was circling above them looking for prey. He had a hard, sharp beak and round dark eyes on either side of his head. His spread-open wings cut through the air like a knife. She was terrified. She wanted to scream, 'Run! Save yourselves. He is going to catch you!' Of course, they could not hear her. She was too far away. But what she saw next changed her life forever.

The rabbit family sat still and waited patiently. Suddenly, when the falcon was on the other edge of the green patch, they jumped, ran as fast as they possibly could, and disappeared into the safety of the tall grass and shrubs.

'What brave rabbits,' she thought. And then an idea appeared in her head. 'Maybe I could be brave too. I am bigger than a rabbit, and how wonderful it would be to not be afraid of everything.'

Martha could not sleep all night and her head was full of thoughts. She really wanted to try to do things by herself but, to do so, she would have to go and face the big, terrifying world. She would need to leave her safe and comfortable cloud. Her heart was pounding but she made her first brave decision. 'I will leave Cloudiotropia to live on earth,' she said to herself.

The next day, Martha carefully packed her carry bag. She took only a few things. One blue dress, her favourite tights with black-and-yellow stripes and a notebook and pen.

She told her mum and dad about her plan. Surprisingly, they looked quite happy when they heard her decision. They only said, 'Be good down there. Be kind to everyone, and if you need us, look up to the sky. We are here for you.'

***

Just to let you know, the Cloudiotropia people can only use rainbows to travel to earth. So, if you see a rainbow in the sky, there is a chance that someone is on the way. Martha had to wait until a rainbow appeared, and when it did, she jumped on and slid down straight into the woods beneath. In that very moment, she felt her body become smaller and smaller, and when she finally touched the ground, she was no taller than a match.

The place where she landed was covered with blueberries and wild strawberries. The green moss was like a soft, thick carpet. There was a toadstool so huge, she could easily find a shelter under it as if it were a big umbrella.

When Martha was on her cloud, she had seen everything from a distance. Now, she could see trees endlessly tall and with sunshine coming through the branches. She heard the sounds of animals and breathed in the scent of flowers. A gentle breeze combed through her hair. However, her braveness disappeared. She felt her heartbeat and could hear

her heavy breathing. She did not know anybody, and she did not know where she should go. So, Martha sat down under the toadstool and started to pretend she was invisible. That always helped her when she was scared.

Suddenly, Martha heard a voice.

'Help, help! Anybody, help me, please!'

She jumped to her feet and ran towards the cry. Finally, she saw a tiny ant in the middle of a puddle. She was sitting on a berry leaf and looking very scared indeed.

'Hello, there. Is there anything I can do for you?' Martha asked.

'Yes, please. I got separated from my fellow ants,' she explained. 'I wanted to find them, and I thought if I could swim across this puddle on the leaf, it would save me a lot of time. Instead, this is what happened to me. I am stuck. The edge is too far, the water is too deep, and I cannot swim. Can you help me, please?'

'Of course I can. Please, wait a minute. I will take my shoes off, and I will bring you to safety,' Martha said.

The ant's name was Lucy. She was the smallest and youngest of the ants. She and her friends had been checking the roads after a storm. Lucy explained to Martha that all roads must be clear for her sisters when they carried food and leaves to the anthill. Martha's new little friend, Lucy, took her to meet her family and even introduced her to the Queen.

Her majesty lived in her own chamber and had a big leaf throne. She was much bigger than the rest of the ants, and she had beautiful silver wings.

The anthill had many tunnels and entrances and looked like a busy town. Everyone had important work to do.

Martha spent some days with them enjoying their company. She explored the woods with Lucy and learnt how to find food – of which the blueberries were the most delicious – how to build shelter, and how to climb flowers. The ants were very busy but kind to her. They had a great time together, but Martha knew that she could not stay there forever.

One sunny day, she said to Lucy, 'My dear Lucy, I think it is time for me to go and find new adventures and friends. I really enjoyed every single day with you. I felt like I was part of your family. You showed me how to take care of myself, and now I know how to find food and build shelter for night-time or rainy days. I would not know these things without you. Thank you for your kindness.'

Lucy was sad about this news, but she understood Martha's decision to leave.

The next day, Martha said goodbye to everyone, and she left her friends from the anthill.

****

The day was beautiful, and the sun was shining in the sky. Martha walked through the glade, passing by tall flowers and grass. Close to noon, she felt a little hungry. Using her new skills, she climbed into a flower to collect the nectar and pollen for lunch. She dipped her head into the flower to reach its sweet drink. Suddenly, Martha felt a movement and heard a deep buzzing sound.

She lifted her head up and realised she was nose to nose with a huge bumblebee. They both screamed in fright.

'I do apologise, my dear. I was not expecting anyone to be here. Are you all right?' the bumblebee asked.

Martha was still shaking but she said slowly, 'Yes, I am fine, thank you. I was just having some lunch.'

'Oh dear, maybe I will leave you alone then as there are plenty of flowers all around. I will find one for me.' He gave her a big smile.

'Stay here, please,' she said. 'This flower is big enough for both of us. I would love to have some company.' Martha could not believe what she had said. It was the first time that she had asked someone to join her.

'Well, if you really do not mind, I will stay. My name is Steve, and this is my field. I work here, taking care of the herbs, flowers, and grass. Do you like it? Do you like my field?' he asked.

'I do. I really, really do,' she replied. 'But what exactly do you do here? I thought that wildflowers do not have to be looked after by anyone. By the way, my name is Martha.' She was surprised by what he had said about his work in the field. She wanted to know more.

He explained to her the importance of his work in detail. She had not known that every single flower, or bush, or tree must be taken care of by bees and other insects. If this did not happen, the plants would die without having the chance to grow again the following year.

'So, you are one of the most important creatures in this world?' she asked, but he shook his head in protest.

11

'No, I do not feel that way about myself. I am just doing what should be done. You see, everyone in this world has a different purpose. We are all doing something important, even if it is a small thing. If one of us stops doing it, the circle of life will be broken. We are like a big chain, all connected, all important. So, I am doing my bit, the flowers are doing their bit, and you are doing yours.'

'But I do not do anything important. I really don't,' Martha said. She was a bit sad because she did not have a purpose.

'I wouldn't be so sure,' said Steve. 'Some of us have the power to change hearts. Maybe that is your purpose, and you don't know it yet?' He gave her a big smile and said, 'I don't give people any advice, but, please, little Martha, give yourself time. I am sure you will find it soon.'

Later, Martha asked if she could help him with his work. He agreed, and for a few hours, they flew from one flower to another, doing simple but important work. At the end of the day, Martha was tired but proud to have helped.

They said their goodbyes and Martha promised him that she would be patient, and she would give herself time to discover what she could do with her life to be helpful. Martha found shelter for the night and went to sleep, thinking that it had been a very good day.

*****

Martha woke the next morning and, as she lay in the grass, watched the sky and the moving clouds. She smiled and at that exact moment, she had the strangest

feeling. She felt as if she knew this place. This field reminded her of something. It somehow looked familiar. She did not know why she felt that way. Suddenly, Martha saw him. It was the falcon; the same one she had seen that day with the rabbit family. He was just right above her with his huge wings. She could not take her eyes from his huge, sharp talons. Martha froze. She did not know what to do. She was afraid he would catch her as his prey.

'Do not move an inch, and be very quiet,' she heard a calm, but firm voice say.

Martha could not see anyone.

'On my signal, get up and run as fast as you possibly can. At the end of this glade are tall shrubs and behind them are the woods. I am on your right side. All right, darling?'

'Uh-huh,' she replied.

'Now! Run with me!' he urged and then Martha saw him for the first time. It was the rabbit – brown, with long ears. They ran at full speed for a while before finally jumping into the shrubs.

'We are safe now,' he said. 'You must be a bit more careful, my love. The clearings can be dangerous if you do not pay attention.'

Martha still could not catch her breath, and all she could say in that very moment was, 'Thank you. You saved me.'

'Not at all,' he said. 'My name is Finnegan. What is your name, my little crumble? And what are you doing here?'

Martha was not sure what to say. Everything had happened so quickly. 'I don't know, actually,' she replied. 'I'm sorry, you asked about my name. My name is Martha, and I am here, because...' She was not sure what to say. 'I am here because I have a rabbit heart, so I am always scared and afraid of everything and everyone.' Somehow this did not come out right. Something had changed in Finnegan's attitude. Martha felt it.

Finnegan raised his left eyebrow and looked at Martha seriously.

'I'm sorry. It wasn't my intention to be rude to you. Will you forgive me?' she asked with her head bowed.

'There is nothing to forgive. I am a rabbit, you know. I know what you are talking about. But let's go. I think it is time for you to meet someone. Shall we?' He showed her the way.

Soon afterwards, they stopped beside a big rabbit hole that was hidden in the tall bushes and grass.

'This is my home and my family; Beatrix, Luis, Maxwell and Trixie. I think we should explain something to you about our rabbit life. But first, lunch! You must be very hungry?'

It was true. Martha had not eaten since the previous night, and now it was almost afternoon.

After lunch, they sat in the shadows and she asked what it was like to be a rabbit. She told them that one day she had seen them and what they had done. Because of that, she had decided to travel to earth and find her courage. She told them about Lucy and Steve, and how they had spent time together.

At the end of the story, Martha said, 'And here I am. I am still the same. I am still frightened, and it seems that nothing has changed.'

All this time, they had listened without saying a word. But then, Finnegan said, 'You see, Martha, you are right about our hearts. They are little, and we are shy, and we are often scared but this is what keeps us alive. We, rabbits, pay attention to what is all around us. We see what is hidden from others. When you are scared, you learn to be cautious and careful. When you are lonely, you learn to appreciate every friendship that is offered to you.

Everything that you are doing is a chance for you to grow your courage. True courage is something that must be learnt, not given. Courage is when you do something for someone. It is when you can help the smallest being, like an ant helping her find the way home, or being gentle and protective of bees. It is these simple, little things that make you brave. Even your jealousy can be useful because through it, you can awaken your dreams, and after that, it is only one step to big and small adventures and finding friends.'

Martha listened with her mouth open. She had never thought about those things in that way. Then, she noticed something strange. A few days ago, she had been the size of Lucy, the ant, but now she was the size of a rabbit. Somehow, Martha had grown since she had come to earth. She was not as fragile and small as she used to be, not anymore. She was still shy and scared like before but now she saw herself in a different way. Martha had tamed her fears and she knew that she could do whatever she wanted to.

Time passed very quickly with Finnegan and his family. They talked and laughed a lot.

Martha heard all about the creatures that lived nearby. She heard about the lady in the lake who Finnegan called The Aquarius. Martha did not notice when night came. She wanted to go and find a shelter for the night, but he insisted that she stay overnight with them. Finnegan's last question to her before he went to sleep was, 'So what are you going to do now, Martha? Are you going to continue your journey on earth?'

She did not know what to say, and Finnegan left her with her thoughts.

The night was quiet, and the moon looked like a big lantern in the sky. Its gentle light touched everything around. For those who were completing their days, it brought rest and dreams. For those who preferred life under the cover of the night, it was like a guide.

Martha watched the plate of a moon for a long time. She thought maybe it was time to go back home to Cloudiotropia. She also thought about what Finnegan had said about the lake nearby and the mysterious lady who lived down there. It had made her curious. Who was she?

Finally, she smiled gently and whispered to herself, 'I miss my home, my cloud, but I want to stay here and know more about my rabbit heart and all the creatures that live here on earth.' Soon after, she fell asleep, kissed by the moonlight.

What happened next, my dear readers, and what new adventures our friend had, are another story about Martha - the girl with a rabbit heart.

Printed in Great Britain
by Amazon

57494953R10015